Goat's Coat

Tom Percival
&
Christine Pym

BLOOMSBURY
CHILDREN'S BOOKS
LONDON OXFORD NEW YORK NEW DELHI SYDNEY

Let me tell you the tale of Alfonzo the goat,
who was terribly proud of his lovely new coat.
It had bright shiny buttons all made out of glass
and a collar the colour of freshly cut grass.

This book is dedicated to
Beatrice Bluebell Panting – T.P.

For my Grandma Barbara,
with love x – C.P.

Coventry City Council	
WHO*	
3 8002 02377 928 5	
Askews & Holts	Apr-2018
	£11.99

BLOOMSBURY CHILDREN'S BOOKS
Bloomsbury Publishing Plc
50 Bedford Square, London, WC1B 3DP, UK

BLOOMSBURY, BLOOMSBURY CHILDREN'S BOOKS and the Diana logo are trademarks of Bloomsbury Publishing Plc
First published in Great Britain by Bloomsbury Publishing Plc

Text copyright © Tom Percival 2018
Illustrations copyright © Christine Pym 2018

Tom Percival and Christine Pym have asserted their rights under the Copyright, Designs and Patents Act, 1988, to be
identified as Author and Illustrator of this work

A catalogue record for this book is available from the British Library

ISBN 978 1 4088 8102 6 (HB)
ISBN 978 1 4088 8101 9 (PB)
ISBN 978 1 4088 8100 2 (eBook)

1 3 5 7 9 10 8 6 4 2

Printed and bound in China by Leo Paper Products, Heshan, Guangdong
All papers used by Bloomsbury Publishing Plc are natural, recyclable products from wood grown in well managed
forests. The manufacturing processes conform to the environmental regulations of the country of origin.

To find out more about our authors and books visit www.bloomsbury.com and sign up for our newsletters

People turned to admire
as Alfonzo walked by.

"What a marvellous coat!"
he heard someone sigh.

Alfonzo was happy – he pranced and he skipped.

Then he heard a sad noise
croaking out of a ditch.

He peered down and found a sad family of frogs –
whose home had once been a mossy old log.

But the log was no more –
it had rotted away.
And the frogs from the log
now had **nowhere** to stay.

The frogs were distraught.
"Please help us!" they cried.

HELP!

And Alfonzo felt sorry for them, so he tried.

He unpicked some stitches from his brand new coat
and, using the fabric, helped make them . . .

. . . a boat.

The frogs were delighted!
He'd just made their day.
"Oh, thank you!" they croaked
as they all sailed away.

Alfonzo's new coat didn't
look quite so smart,
but he felt a warm glow
in the depths of his heart.

He clipped on and on till he came to a shed –
the sound from within filled Alfonzo with dread.

What could possibly make
such a sad sound as that?

Alfonzo peered in,
then he saw it . . .

. . . a cat.

The cat was trembling and terribly pale.
It was clear to see that
she'd hurt her tail.

Alfonzo got busy
and cleaned up the cut.

Then, using his coat,
he bandaged it up.

The cat was so glad,
so grateful and happy,
but Alfonzo's new coat was
now looking quite tatty.

He clip-clopped along
through the crisp winter's day.
He was whistling a song
when a hen came his way.

The hen was upset – she'd lost one of her chicks.
Might this be something Alfonzo could fix?

Together the hen and Alfonzo looked round . . .

but the hen's little chick
just couldn't be found.

From somewhere up high
a voice cried, "Help meeeeee!"
And there was the chick
stuck up in a tree.

So Alfonzo removed **even more** of his coat . . .

and tied it together
to make a long rope.

He climbed up the tree
just as fast as a rocket!

And then he came down
with the chick in his pocket.

Alfonzo's new coat was now looking a mess.
Still, what's done is done – it was all for the best.

As Alfonzo walked on
there were more
problems still . . .

but he helped solve them all
with his coat and his skill.

Alfonzo's new coat
was now just a few threads,

but he smiled as he thought
of his good deeds instead.

The weather grew colder –
snow fell all around.
Poor coatless Alfonzo trudged
back towards town.

The blizzard grew worse –
it got **colder** and **colder**.
Alfonzo took shelter
behind a large boulder.

Alfonzo was **freezing**
and night would soon fall,
so, there, he curled up
in a cold little ball.

But then he heard voices
ring out through the night.
Someone was shining
a welcoming light.

He spotted the **frogs**
and the **cat** and the **hen**!

He wasn't alone –
he'd been found
by his friends.

Seeing them all made
Alfonzo feel better
and, not only that,
they had brought him . . .

. . . a sweater!

They had made it themselves
from the things
they could find . . .

. . . A gift to Alfonzo
for being so kind.

And so our dear goat had
made **best friends** forever.
And he wore his new sweater
whatever the weather.